POTTY POWER!

Scan this code on your smart phone to download DC Super Friends activity sheets.

Alternatively, visit
www.randomhousechildrens.co.uk/dc-superfriends

BANTAM

™ & © DC Comics. (s14)

"Time to become a big super hero and get rid of those nappies," Superman tells Sam. The Man of Steel blows them all away with a mighty breath.

"To defeat nappies, you'll have to master your potty powers!"

"What Sam needs now is a plan," Batman tells Robin. The two of them check to see that Sam has everything he needs.

How will Sam know when it's time? He'll have to **listen** to his body.

Suddenly, his body starts to feel **wiggly.** Is that the signal?

When should you listen for **your** signal?

Listen while you play . . .

Listen while you read . . .

Listen while you watch TV . . .

Listen and you will know when it's time to . . .

Sam races to the bathroom. The Flash can use his super-speed to go anywhere on the Earth in seconds. Sam is fast too, but not that fast!

"Don't wait to go until the last minute," The Flash says. "Give yourself enough time to get where you need to be."

Will Sam make it?

YES! Sam made it to the bathroom where he can go using his potty powers! He is one step closer to defeating nappies. But he's not done yet!

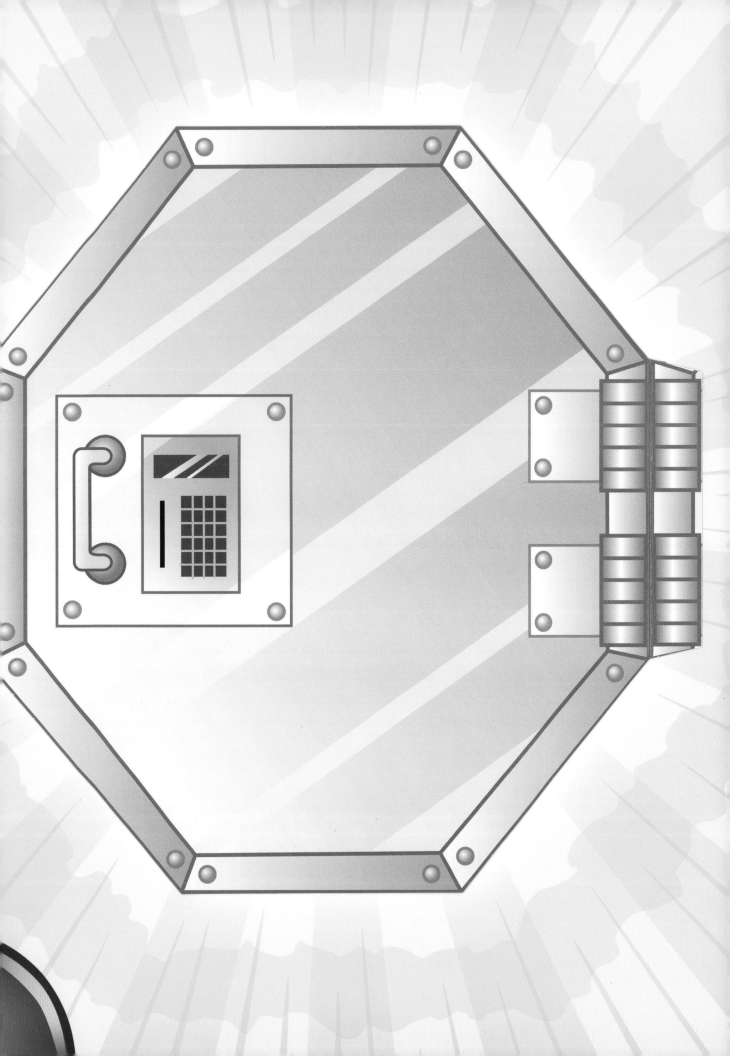

"There's one more thing to do," Aquaman tells Sam. "When you're finished, you need to use the power of water to flush the toilet and wash your hands."

Sam learns that washing his hands with soap and water helps him battle bad germs and stay healthy.

It's time to give Sam a sticker!

"You did it!" Sam's Super Friends cheer. Sam feels proud and now he's a **real** hero. He's ready to fly off on another adventure. Let's go!

My Potty Training Reward Chart

Add a reward sticker every time you use your potty powers!

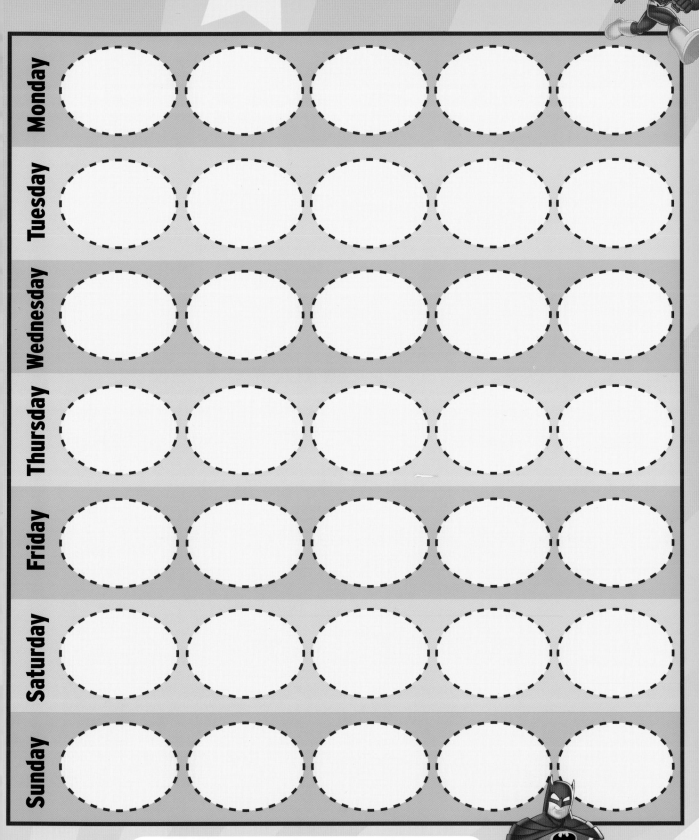

Monday					
Tuesday					
Wednesday					
Thursday					
Friday					
Saturday					
Sunday					

This reward chart is reusable; so you can use it again and again!

My Potty Training Reward Chart

Add a reward sticker every time you use your potty powers!

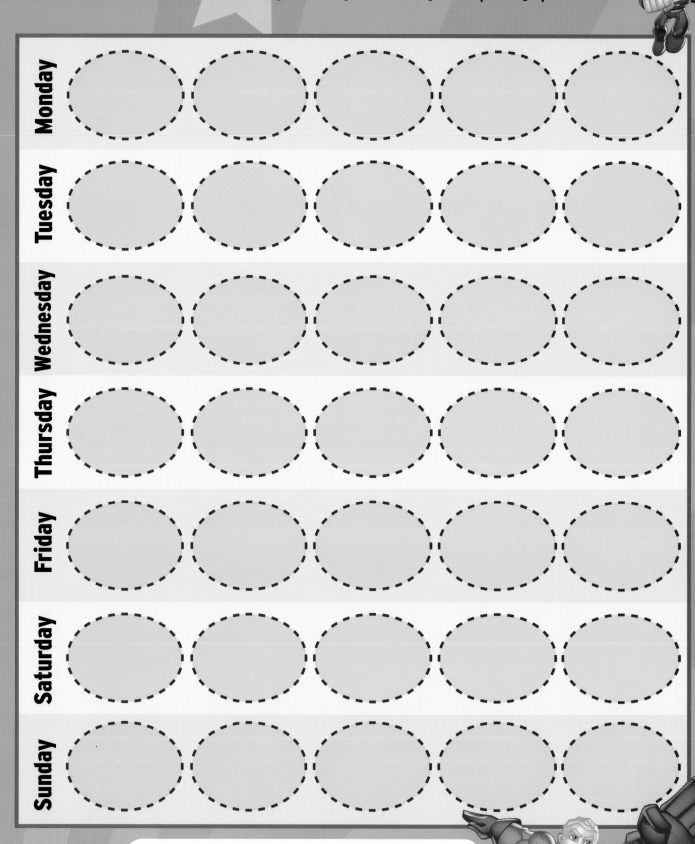

Monday

Tuesday

Wednesday

Thursday

Friday

Saturday

Sunday

This reward chart is reusable; so you can use it again and again!

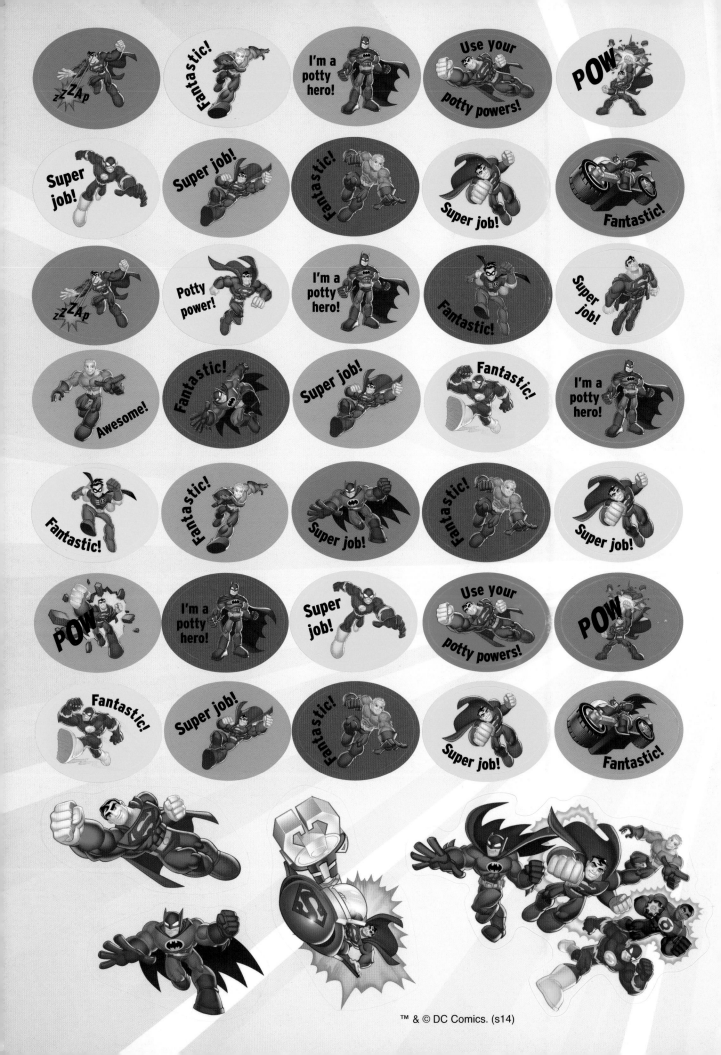